...all good

apologies end

in a #ashtag

BRIAN WILCOX

ISBN: 978-1-7346118-0-9

HEW Publishing
L L C

DEDICATION

To my family

CONTENTS

Acknowledgments   1

"The Third Sandwich"   4

"You've Got a Friend"   8

"The Audience"   28

"Never Say Die"   57

"Flattening the Curve"   72

"Ghostwriter"   77

"Denominators"   78

"The Power of Persuasion"   80

"A Snapshot of You Doing the Dishes"   81

"A Stranger in Home Depot"   82

"Vintage"   83

"Perhaps"   84

"She"   85

"Moss"   86

"The Most Terrifying Feeling in the World"   87

CONTENTS

"Patience Standing Still"   88

"A Second"   89

"Crane"   90

"Complicate"   91

"The First Time"   92

"…all good apologies end in a #ashtag"   93

"Four A.M. on the Sand"   95

"When I am Old"   97

"Pedagogy"   99

"Adventures of a Selfie"   101

"Sordid View"   102

"Still Awakening"   104

"Salute"   105

"Chance"   106

"Hiding Away in the Inside of Jacket"   108

"Everyone Else was Grieving"   109

CONTENTS

"Milestone #3"   111

"Addiction"   112

"Ligature"   113

"Four Pages in March"   114

"Blackout"   115

"Frame"   116

"Bridges"   118

"Independence Day"   119

"In a Hoarder's Living Room in Connecticut"   122

"Parallel Lines and Structures"   125

"The Humble Horizon with Then and Now"   127

"Parados"   129

"Umbrella"   130

ABOUT THE AUTHOR   131

ACKNOWLEDGMENTS

With thanks to the many people, colleagues, students, teachers, friends, family, animals and others that have provided some sort of inspiration along the way.

Thank you…

...all good

apologies end

in a #ashtag

"The Third Sandwich"

A Play in One Act

It is a brisk, winter morning as the sunlight begins to peer from a dark, cloudy sky in a crowded condominium parking lot. Three cars; one a dark-colored, new Toyota Camry, one an indistinct aging Hyundai, and one a still older, dirty Ford Fusion stir in adjacent parking spaces; idling, warming up — carbon-monoxide permeating the stillness of the dawn. A tall, awkward man in his mid-twenties emerges from the condominium, running and frantically waving a zip-lock bag containing a sandwich; the wires of a pair of white earbuds wildly wafting through the air.

Man: Your sandwich!

An awkward woman with glasses in her mid-twenties reluctantly rolls down the window in the defrosting Toyota Camry. She has dressed monochromatically in a pair of khaki pants and an ill-fitting, loose beige blouse.

Man: — *gesticulating excitedly:* Your sandwich!

Woman: — *barely audible:* I've got mine…

Man: — *angrily waving the sandwich:* YOUR SANDWICH!

Woman: — *louder:* I have my sandwich!

Man: — *shocked:* What? That's not possible. This is yours!

Woman: No! I have mine.

Man: —*angry that he is questioned:* No, this is yours!

Woman: — *agitated:* Do you seriously want me to check and prove it to you?

Man: — *with emphasis:* Yes! This is your sandwich! I have mine!

Woman: Fine. I'll get my lunch box and prove it to you. — *The woman gets out of the car, looks angrily at the man, dramatically turns, opens the rear driver-side door, and emerges with a pink, canvas lunch box. She unzips the lunch box and holds it up with concomitant triumph and disdain at the man:* Look, I have my sandwich. Are you satisfied now?

The woman and lunch box reenter the driver side door of the Toyota followed by an emphatic slam that elicits an air of superiority and sense of self. The window remains open.

Man: — *shocked:* How can this be? I have my sandwich and you have yours. Were there three sandwiches?

Woman: — *suddenly confused:* Can't be. Are you sure you have yours? Why would there be three sandwiches?

Man: — *furious:* Yes! I told you I have mine. Why would I lie about having my sandwich? – *with a need to prove himself:* Wait, I'll get my lunch box and show you.

The man turns abruptly mumbling into the daybreak without soliciting a response and re-enters the condominium.

Woman: — *flabbergasted and speaking introspectively:* You don't need to -- *She stops as the man leaves. To herself* -- Fine.

Almost before the flimsy screen door can wind shut, the condominium door opens with intensity and the man reappears with a large, open lunch box displaying a flimsy sandwich of Wonder Bread with processed meats and cheeses, a snack-size bag of plain Lays potato chips, and a bulging Tupperware container of carrots and celery. No dressing or dipping options. It is the single most boring lunch in human history.

Man: — *with a simultaneous sense of pride and complete bewilderment.* Look! I told you I had my sandwich. So there are three of them? – *pauses to contemplate:* Three sandwiches? I don't understand how this could be. I made my sandwich. You made your sandwich. Who made the third sandwich? Seriously. Why is there a third sandwich?

Woman: — *truly puzzled and with a sudden change from anger to compassion:*
I have no idea.

Man: I'm so confused.

The man secures his lunch box, shrugs dejectedly with defeat, and reenters the condominium. The woman pauses in anxious thought while examining the gleaming diamond clung tightly around her finger, rolls up her window, and slowly backs out of her parking space into the hazy morning, sandwich-enclosed lunch box held safely by her side.

The man reemerges, without animation, into the brisk morning, lunch box in banded hand, and climbs into his aging Hyundai before backing out with hesitation and regret.

Following the man and woman's exit, inside the salt-stained Ford Fusion, a neighbor, reassured, turns up the radio and laughs at the random folly of life.

#neighbors #idlingcarsandbattlescars

"You've Got a Friend"

"Thank you so much, Mom! Really, you have outdone yourself."

"Thank you, honey. Are you sure you don't want to just stay here? It's late, it's Christmas, and it has to be at least a few hours back to the apartment. It's no bother!"

"No, no. We absolutely need to get going," as the strains of the 17th repetition of Perry Como's "Home for the Holiday's" filled the air.

We hurriedly walked to the car and with that, we left. Michelle and I crammed the exorbitant amount of gifts into the backseat of "Bert," her beloved Chevy, and started the trek back to her apartment. It was the newest, old car I had ever seen. One of those cars that looks dated while new on the lot. It was a so-called sub-compact; it was the color of old mustard in the sun, and GM had dubbed it the "Vega" after the brightest star in some constellation.

Marketing at its absolute finest. This car was no star, that's for sure, and possessed no "stellar" qualities. It's made even more ridiculous that Michelle had given the Vega its nickname after Bert, the most boring and disturbing character from the Muppets. Seriously, if there was a car that would collect paper clips and bottle caps then it was this one.

I had been staying at her apartment since graduation as we figured out what the next step would be. It was about a four-hour drive but we had made this trek quite a few times already. It was typically a pretty boring ride so a third voice from the radio was an absolute necessity during those moments of quietude.

The roads were icy, yet passable as I turned onto the ramp for I-70. Only four more hours to go, I thought to myself. Music. Please, music. I turned the dial. "Silent Night." "Jingle Bells." "O Holy Night?" Well, that could work. One more turn.

"Santa Claus was Coming to Town." Such a disturbing song.

"Christmas music everywhere. David, please, I cannot deal with any more Christmas music."

"I know, I know. Wait, Rock 95 should be good," as I aggressively turned the dial away from forced holiday spirit. "There it is."

I dialed the radio in, finally finding something that would least give us a soundtrack for the beginning of our journey.

"Really? Donna Summer brought back "Macarthur Park"? And how is this on a rock station?" Michelle pondered.

Legitimate questions. I thought for a second. "Well, it's disco but not disco. It's got to be on its way out, right? Either way. It's a sad song. Cake is delicious. And this one was out in the rain and now the icing is melted or something. It's the great American tragedy, no? We all want our cake; and to eat it, too. It hits me right here," I said dramatically pointing to my stomach.

You're an idiot," Michelle correctly asserted. "But, at least we're on our way now. I love your family, I do. But…" She paused to find the right words. "That roast is like eating a football. I get it. Nobody wants trichinosis and especially you do not want to be the supplier of undercooked meat. But, I mean there's got to be a happy medium, no? There's no amount of cranberry sauce to give that pork any flavor."

She wasn't wrong and I was just as glad to be leaving, too. Albeit for other reasons. The highway was desolate and the snow had picked up in intensity. Most people were either at home celebrating or had determined to not brave the elements. The lack of lighting on the freeway was a separate issue to confront. Aside from a random plow here or there, there was a total absence of life on this Christmas evening.

"Time for a new song. That yellow dress, green icing? That poor man playing Chinese Checkers? Get that guy Trouble or Twister or something," I joked.

I spun the dial again.

Ahh, "Le Freak." Nice. I can admit that this is nice. Disco or not.

"Umm, what's that sound?" Michelle appeared concerned.

"Nile Rodgers, baby!" I exclaimed. Most underrated rhythm guitarist ever! "Did you know the original words were supposed to be "Fuck Off" instead of "Freak Out? Should've stayed with the f-bomb," I remarked. "Makes it edgier."

"No, David. I thought I heard a noise from the car. Turn the radio down."

"Michelle, you cannot turn this down. That's blasphemy. It's JCs birthday. Let him get a little funky. Besides, I didn't feel anything. Must've hit a little snowpack or it's probably just the vibe of the night. An empty highway, snow, no lights. Christmas? It's enough to make you hear things."

In attempting to reassure her, I was actually concerning myself. In resignation, I turned down the radio. There was a noise. It was faint, but it was there. Metallic. A grinding sound that seemed to be getting more prevalent.

"Shit, I hear it, too."

It was one of the moments where the senses work together but in contradictory ways. Synesthesia? I think that's what it's called. As I heard the subtle, yet consistent grating from the engine, I began to sense the Vega losing a little something. With each sound, rising in complexity and dread, the RPMs slowed just enough to become ever more noticeable.

"C'mon, Bert!" Michelle was yelling, "Not now, please, not now!"

The engine whirred angrily as we narrowly averted stalling traversing a slow incline. I kept on thinking, this is the Midwest, and the shit's supposed to be flat. As we would crest the hill, I would

carefully downshift and try to build up speed to lighten the load on

the engine. But the further we went, the louder the sound became.

"How Deep is Your Love" began to serenade us at the

absolute worst possible moment.

"Oh, shut the fuck up, Barry!" Michelle exclaimed. "Not this

song. Not now!"

I quickly turned the dial away from the Brothers Gibb and

landed on a clear station. How apropos.

Wings permeated the air waves as the cool, funky section of

"Band on the Run" instructed us on what to do if we survived this

"place."

I tried to calm Michelle down with my patented not so funny

or appreciated humor.

"Hmm, well the song fits. Although I still blame Paul and

Linda for the way everything went down. People want to blast Yoko

all the time. And I mean, sure, she sucks. But Paul deserves more

than his fair share of the blame. Poor Lennon nearly gets deported by

the INS, but Paul is somehow just allowed to go on his own magical

mystery tour?"

"Are you seriously bringing this up now? Really? Michelle was not appreciating my humorous soothing.

"Just trying to bring some levity," I sheepishly replied, knowing that my timing was, as usual, pretty terrible.

I was trying not to panic, but there was so little I could do. My knowledge of car maintenance was minimal. I could change a tire. I could check a dipstick like a pro. "Always keep an old rag under the hood," my old man proclaimed. But this was far out of my headspace especially in this setting, time of night, and the inclement weather conditions. The car continued to slow and stall as any acceleration was required and I knew that the safest thing to do was the terrifically unsafe decision to pull onto the shoulder, on a dark highway in the middle of nowhere, in an ever-increasing snowstorm no less, and try to seek help.

"What are you doing? You're pulling over? Here? Now? What are we going to do?" Michelle worriedly yelled. She was starting to panic.

"Listen, we're better off just pulling over than getting stuck on a hill or stalling out in the middle of the highway when another car would not be able to see us. I'm going to try to get to a straightaway so we could flag someone down. It's probably a two-mile walk to the next exit and then God knows how long to a service station. And they're probably all closed anyway. Merry Christmas to us."

"We should have just stayed at your mom's," Michelle was beginning to worry especially with a statement as irrational as that.

"Well, we can't do anything about that now. We're what, maybe an hour from Novi or so? Maybe we can just find someone to get a lift into the next town or something. We'll find a pay phone and we can call Jenny or Rob and they can come and get us. We don't have many other options here, 'Chelle. We'll be alright. Trust me."

I was trying to convince myself as much as she was. But it was affirming even if it was a form of self-assurance. After slowing to only around 20 miles an hour, still losing speed, I found a decent straight away and slowly lurched the car onto the shoulder. I hadn't seen another car in probably 15 minutes, because, you know, they were smart not to be out and about in this. In considering our options, I was thinking we might have to just spend the night in ole' Bert.

We were probably an hour or so outside Detroit now, but at least we would have music as a compatriot. Michelle and I waited and waited but there were zero cars on the highway at this time of night. I further considered my options. Do I leave her here in the car to go and find help? Do we both go? Do we hope that Auntie Grace's crocheting skills on her quilts (bless you, cheap handmade gift) would suffice to survive a sub-freezing Michigan night? As the myriad of possibilities ran through my head, some good, most bad, I scantily saw a beacon of hope in two white-washed, faded headlights slowly making their way towards us. The car was an old one, you could tell by the front face and silhouette, and was moving cautiously through the speckled white horizon.

"Someone's coming, 'Chelle! Give me something to get their attention!"

Michelle grabbed a newly opened Christmas gift: a set of hideously tacky, powder blue monogrammed towels, and hastily handed them to me as I did my best Pittsburgh Steelers fan impersonation by waving them wildly about my head. Terrible Towel indeed.

"Help, please!" I yelled repeatedly into the dark, brisk night fully knowing that whoever was in that car was not going to be able to see me.

The car seemed to notice us as it gradually slowed on the glistening asphalt and came to a stop some 30 yards north of us. The parking lights illuminated the dark highway and the car perilously paused as if the driver were expecting me to run to his aid. I will admit that I was ecstatic to find help but also concerned by this initial encounter. After a good minute or so, I began to carefully jog through the snow encumbered shoulder towards our rescuer when I noticed a solitary white light emerge from the rear of the car as it ever so leisurely backed toward Michelle and me. The second backup light was out.

Coming to a final stop about 10 feet from me, I noticed the driver-side window of the vehicle slowly crank open. It was an old Pontiac Catalina, probably from the early 60s or so, with a myriad of dents and a distinctive rust color that was ambiguously both the coloration of the body and the gradual disintegration of the integrity of the car.

Walking with purpose yet hesitation, I approached the window as a large cloud from a Macanudo Cigar engulfed my snow-stained face.

"What seems to be the problem, guy?"

The voice was gravelly and pensive. The voice intimated concern more for our story than our current situation.

"The car just died. Stallin' up the hills and no power. We've got another hour or so to get to Novi and we're stuck out here. Please tell me you are a mechanic or know cars or something," I pleaded.

"Cars? Me? Nope. Look at this thing," He gestured toward the Pontiac. "I just put the gas in and hope for the best. This one's been through some adventures."

He was a strange man. Eye contact was not his forte and the only distinguishing facial feature I could make out was the thick mutton chops that dominated his profile. It was difficult to even ascertain an age range based on his lack of personal connection.

In desperation, after a period of silence, I finally just went for it.

"So…. Could we catch a lift? My girlfriend's in the car and we're just trying to get back to her apartment. Please? I can throw a couple of bones your way for your trouble. Maybe just to a payphone or something."

"Sure. Best hurry though. The weather the way it is, things could just get worse for you two the longer you are here. Grab your girl. We'll see what we can do."

I ran back to ole' Bert and filled Michelle in on the situation. In my peripheral vision, I saw the Catalina backing up closer to us.

"Let's go," I implored. "This is our best bet. This guy is a little strange but harmless. What other option do we have?"

We grabbed as much as we could from the Vega and started filling up the stranger's car with our bags and Christmas gifts. I was still struck by the complete lack of eye contact or personalization as the aged smell of Macanudo filled the car.

"You got a lot of presents. Nice. People love you, that's nice," the mutton-chopped stranger proclaimed. "Best take all you can. Wouldn't want someone to come by and take what was not there's. Those people are out here, you know."

Cryptic feeling though it was, Michelle and I climbed into the front seat of the car. They were bucket seats; three-wide and I decided it would be best for me to sit in the middle just in case. As I was sitting, I began playing out the various scenarios of taking a ride from this man.

He turned the volume up on this antiquated radio and we listened, disheartened, as the Stockholm met Mr. Fitzgerald.

We set off slowly down 75. The road conditions had deteriorated considerably and there was a strange, convergent feeling of relief and terror simultaneously overtaking me. We were saved from our broken down Vega, but now we were entrusting our safety to a man whose mysterious manner just may have been a more concerning endeavor than our previous situation.

The music continued to play as the three of us sat in abject silence on the darkened highway. Michelle shared several concerning glances with me but all I could do was shrug my shoulders. We were headed in the right direction, the Catalina was performing admirably, and our luck, finally, seemed to be improving.

Still, our mysterious driver remained silent. After many minutes of total stillness, our driver began the first treatise on his dissertation on the decline of human decency.

"You two are just lucky I came along. There's a lot of sickos out there. They're everywhere. Especially this time of night on a dark highway? Whoa boy, there's no telling just who is a friend or a foe anymore."

As he completed his statement, he removed one hand from the steering wheel and started searching for something under his seat. After several attempts, a wry, concerning smile came across his face.

"Here," he was holding a Smith and Wesson snub-nosed .38 Special lovingly in his right hand. "There she is."

I instinctively moved closer to Michelle to concomitantly shield her and attempt to get some distance from the revolver that was now pointed at us at point-blank range.

"That's why I carry this. If you encounter me and you are not a friend? Well, I've got this to stand my ground and protect myself from those who are not nice."

"Look," I said, "We want no trouble. We were just looking for some help."

"Oh, I know," he said as his hand waved the gun back and forth, "You two are friends of mine now and I can see that you mean ME no harm." He laughed uneasily.

After a short time caressing the firearm, he slowly replaced the .38 in his covert spot underneath the seat, switched the radio station, and then placed his right hand into its correct 10 o'clock position as we continued on our way.

The conversation was intermittent as we made our way past Detroit towards Novi. Our driver's words were ambiguous as he elaborated on the inherent danger of the "stranger" while subsequently confirming the luck of his arrival. Our fears somewhat assuaged, Michelle and I began our next plan of action.

Much to our surprise, we were taken right to Michelle's doorstep. Now a little after midnight, we disembarked from the car and for the first time got a legitimate look at our ghostly, highway savior. He was a large, scruffy man of probably 35, and I was astonished that he insisted on helping us move the gifts from the Catalina into Michelle's apartment.

"I can't thank you enough, um, I'm sorry; I don't think I ever got your name?"

"Odyn. No sweat, Chief. Just gotta be careful if you go back out there. That highway is no place to get stuck."

"Yeah, I hear you. Thanks again, Odyn. Here." I handed him some cash not expecting him to take it, but he gladly accepted.

Odyn held out his hand and I was astonished at the rough condition of his skin. These were well-used hands; covered with cuts, calluses, and dried dirt.

"Be easy, Chief." Odyn climbed into the Catalina, turned up the volume on the radio, and deliberately drove off into the darkness as "Seasons in the Sun" overtook the solitude of the night.

I turned to Michelle.

"Jesus, that was a hell of a trip. For a second, I thought the worst about ole' Mutton Chop there. Could you believe he pulled his piece out? Listen, let's get some sleep, and then we'll call Jen in the morning to give us a ride out to the Vega. We can call a wrecker to meet us out there and then get a lift to the service station and take it from there."

Michelle was clearly shaken but she obliged and we very quickly drifted off to sleep.

With the sunrise, Michelle called her best friend Jen to haul us out to the car on 75. Jen reluctantly agreed and came by to take us out to the interstate.

"Must've been some trip," Jen opined. "I can't believe you just took a ride from such a strange man on the highway. What if he was some psycho killer or something? Can you imagine that? Christmas night, empty highway, a snowstorm? It's like a clichéd Stephen King storyline."

"The thought certainly crossed our mind," Michelle added. But after some awkwardness, in the beginning, he was actually kind of friendly. Don't you think, David?"

"Aside from the gun… yeah," I laughed.

Jen looked at us as if we were joking and turned on the radio, but our eyes told a different story.

"I don't know about this new guy, Perry. Steve Perry? I think that's his name. I liked the early Journey. You know with Gregg and Neil doing their thing. Now it's all mainstream and polished. Oh well."

Jen had a habit of elucidating every thought regardless of how incomprehensible or irreverent it may be. Out on 75, the snow had, for the most part, melted and our mustard-colored Vega was resting patiently on the shoulder awaiting our arrival.

"Tow is en-route, Jen. You can just drop us off. Thank you so much for your help. We'll ride in with the driver to Sovels over on West 10 Mile. Hope it's a simple fix."

Jen drove off quickly down the highway as I shook my head.

"My turn, 'Chelle. Thank god she's gone. I swear, if I had to listen to one more word, I was going to lose it."

Michelle mustered a mocking laugh while I walked to the car to wait for the tow.

"What the… 'Chelle, the back window is broken! Someone else was here last night. Look, they stole a bunch of stuff, too. Random stuff. That sweater and the Emmylou Harris record? Jesus. Keep 'em. Wait, they took those freakin' towels? They're gone, too. Man, whatever pirates busted in last night must be pretty disappointed with their booty. Serves 'em right, bastards. Well, at least we took most of the good stuff home with us last night with Mutton Chop. Hey, here comes the tow."

The wrecker pulled in front of us and slowly backed up to the Vega. Michelle and I were rummaging through the ransacked gifts when we heard the driver yell to us to get into the passenger side of the wrecker to be protected from oncoming traffic. His back was to us and I watched as he unwound the various tow chains and prepared to hook Bert up to the truck bed. He was a large man bedecked in overalls, a trucker's cap, and a light blue towel crammed into the back pocket. Michelle and I sat down and were immediately overcome with the stench of stale cigar smoke.

"Jeez, I guess we're in for another smoky ride," Michelle sarcastically quipped. "Never thought I'd yearn to be surrounded by someone chain-smoking Winston's instead. I just cannot wait for all of this to be over with, David. Worst Christmas ever. I just want to get Bert fixed and get ready for New Years' to drink off the memory of this holiday."

I heard the hydraulics come to life as Bert was lifted onto the wrecker relieved that this was all coming to an end. I looked at Michelle and our eyes met as I attempted to console her and reassure her that this was just another random adventure in our lives.

"Listen, shit happens. The car will be fine. We are fine. Sure, someone broke the back window and stole some useless stuff but it's all going to be cool. Just think… It's a story to tell our kids one day.

Perry Como, the Bee Gees, Mutton Chop, and overcooked pork. All the components are there," I laughed.

I looked back to see the driver, back still turned to us, putting the final touches onto the tow. Michelle and I again locked glances as the driver hopped behind the wheel.

"Seriously, it's all going to be fine," as I reached over to hug Michelle.

"How about some music, folks?" the driver said from his now open door as the eerily subdued acoustic guitar of James Taylor shattered the quiet of the moment.

It was "You've Got a Friend."

I told you, you just never know when you're gonna find a friend or a foe."

I let go of Michelle as I saw his hand go under the seat...

#christmassongsforthesoul #gotfriendsincoldplaces

"The Audience"

We were called *The Audience*. A sometimes good, at times completely solid, bordering on mediocre original band from New London, CT who played rock music that rocked, or at least that is how we liked to portray it. Some of us had big dreams; some of us wanted to play music to express ourselves, some of us simply wanted to get laid. However you frame it, it was quite an experience.

Amazingly, the cast of characters external to the band is sometimes even more impressive to those internally. True randomness personified with a heaping side of memory.

It has been almost 10 years since it all began but I find myself, now, just now, feeling as though I could place these moments into writing. To give them substance, to give them appreciation, and to paint them as vividly and strangely as they occurred all those years ago in a space of time that I neither truly appreciated nor completely understood. What follows is a trip down memory lane, a jaunt through the toils of being minor musicians with egos too large, characters whose mere mention brings up a myriad of bizarre imagery, and a journey through a bevy of experiences. Equal parts sublime, equal parts strange, yet entirely memorable.

CLINT

I first met Clint in my junior year of college in the spring of 2001 on an UConn Bus. He was a year older than I was and he just had this genial presence about him. At first, I was unsure what to think of him as I could not tell if he was a "hanger-on," a sycophant, or one of the most magnetic people I've ever met. His love of music was infectious and although he was a novice songwriter and guitarist (at the time,) I was drawn to his passion. He was constantly working, tweaking, and honing his ever-growing array of songs, and his ambition, sense of humor, timing, and persona rubbed off on all those who encountered him. He's a truly unique human being. All these years later, he still is.

We first played together in the seminal version of Picasso Jelly at the University of Connecticut. While not a member of the original incarnation, I had joined the band fairly early on and was present for most of the highlights.

Picasso Jelly was an original rock band fueled by non-verbal dysfunction. The thing is, though, is that we were usually very good. Dumo, the other guitarist, was an outstanding musician with an incredible ear and vast musical sphere of influence. Hurta, the bassist, has an incredible voice. And Sadi, the drummer, quite possibly the funniest person I have ever met. Almost immediately we connected as a band and wrote some really cool, yet different music. Songs that still sound relevant despite their being now, over twenty years-old.

Along the ride we had many great moments performing at incredible venues in front of multitudes of people; me as a guitarist, Clint as a jack of all trades singer, guitarist, keyboardist, and airport public address announcer. The other bandmates were a who's who of Connecticut legends. The term legend is used obviously, extremely loosely. The faces constantly changed but names such as Tony Testo, John Cusack, Landon, Lawyer Devin, Bauermann, Scuba Steve, Reuben, Jimmy the Greek, not one but two Romano brothers, "Can't Stand Ya'" Senez, and numerous attractive female vocalists rounded out the roving band of misfits that surrounded Clint and me during the various incarnations of Picasso Jelly.

Our first rehearsal space was in a large frat house off campus where we would occasionally gig. This was convenient but as always this momentary advantage was lost when Sadi, an SAE brother, went AWOL. In a total bind, we took on a new drummer - the inimitable Tony Testo.

TESTO

Tony was probably in his 40s when I first met him. He could have been older. It was really difficult to tell. He lived alone in a large house in Monroe, CT with an endless collection of dogs, an angry ferret, and a six-foot iguana named Jub-Jub.

Tony was a good drummer although he was prone to doing very strange things behind the set rhythmically but I do have to say he was quite a host for allowing us such access to his home. While annoying, we would often make weekends out of our rehearsal schedule and stay at Tony's home crashing where we fell with an understanding that whoever had their girlfriend for the night, would receive a private bedroom to get laid.

These rehearsals are legendary in our minds. A cramped room in the basement, endless McDonald's double cheeseburgers (49¢!), incredibly cheap booze, and Jub-Jub emerging into the practice room to shit on the floor near the end of the practice session. I swear he would only shit during one specific song, but perhaps that detail is exaggerated.

Still, Picasso Jelly had a nice little run. We gigged all over CT and drew pretty solid crowds with a highlight being a three coach-bus packed crew from UConn filling the Webster Theater that got us a decent amount of publicity through the *Hartford Advocate* and via word of mouth with club owners. A fitting juxtaposition was being booted to accommodate an UConn women's basketball game on the big screen. How the mighty do fall!

Testo eventually started dating a beautiful teenage girl who was attending Boston College and she, perhaps for good reason, took up most of his time. He would often just leave us to man his large home while he drove her to and from BC. The arrangement as constituted was strange and only got stranger. With the graduation of three of the other members, that ridiculous run ceremoniously and without any fanfare, was over.

Following college, most of the names went their separate ways into the annals of reality. Dumo, rightfully so, is making a living in the music world in Nashville. The real world claimed Hurta and regulated him to weekend warrior status, Devin became an attorney, Scuba Steve, Sadi, Reuben, and the Romano brothers continued down their path into career and family, and only God knows where Testo or Cusack ended up. If you ever read this, Testo, thanks for the hospitality!

Clint and I stuck together determined to give the musician life another go. Yet again, we assembled a cast to toss our hat into the ring. Given the symbolism of the time, we decided to finally rename the band and start fresh. Any person who has faced the task of developing a new band name will tell you that indeed it is an arduous and for a lack of more imaginative adjectives, a stupid task. During the Picasso Jelly days during extreme moments of inebriation and altered consciousness, we developed an ever-growing number of possible names. Sadi had a list of over 100 with my personal favorite,

Cornering Helga. Always though, *The Audience* was a favorite amongst the list.

The Audience was officially formed in 2002 with me on guitar, Clint on guitar and vocals, Dimitri (aka Jimmy the Greek) on bass, and Matt "Mastro" Mastronunzio on drums. With a few old Picasso Jelly songs and a bunch of new material, it was the beginning of a ridiculous ride culminating in a surreal few months in the "Whaling City," New London, CT.

MASTRO

Our first drummer's name was Matt Mastronunzio; Mastro for short. He was a tall, skinny, ultra-intense individual who resembled a crazed spider monkey behind the kit. Arms and legs flailed against an invisible force. Spasmodic flurries of drum fills came at inopportune times and dynamics were but a mere suggestion.

His technique and repertoire were unlike any drummer I have ever played within the manner that he simply had no formality to anything that he did. No beat, fill, or piece of musical expression was ever repeated. No idea or structure was remembered and simply stated, you never knew what the fuck he was apt to do. Every time you played with him, you felt as though it were, in fact, the very first time. It was at once, concomitantly, liberating, and completely terrifying.

Clint and I had first encountered Mastro at UConn when Matt was the lead singer in a "trip-hop" band called *Psycloptics*. They mixed very solid musicianship intermingled with incredibly juvenile lyrics. Jokingly referred to as "Colostomy Bag" by the drunken wheelchair guy at Villa on the Hill, I was astonished when it turned out that Mastro would be the original drummer of The Audience given that he was, you know, not a drummer.

As it is with all drummers, or so it seems, Mastro brought along considerable baggage. His girlfriend was a ticking time bomb, and dealing with her and her "entourage" left you constantly on your toes. If she was not in an overly amorous, medicated, or inebriated state, then she took the paradoxical stance of being psychotically violent. On one occasion, she was wanted for attempting to stab Mastro and at other points was suspected of stealing various items from our gigs, including our own stuff. Nights, when she would bring friends, would result in further issues. I vividly remember one night, post-show, at Mastro's apartment with his friend, the one and only, DJ Screwface. Mastro's girlfriend was being sought by the police for her latest escapade and in the extreme throes of drunkenness, Screwface was going full interventionist. I don't believe in all that much, but when someone named DJ Screwface is lecturing you about how fucked up your relationship is, you should probably listen and take heed to the wisdom therein. In retrospect, this was one of the last times I spoke to Mastro.

Anyways, our initial rehearsals occurred at Mastro's parents' house in Montville, CT. A beautiful house with a deadly steep driveway, we would rehearse once or twice a week to hone our craft and develop many of the songs that Clint and I had been playing and writing since the Picasso Jelly days as well as some newer material.

Initially, rehearsals were very rough. Mastro, while talented, was a novice drummer and he took quite a while to get up to speed. His hip/hop background afforded us moments of free-styled drumming musical genius that often ever so quickly faded away into a cacophonous abyss.

But over time, we had something - I'm not sure what it was, but it was something.

––

DIMITRI

Dimitri was initially the bassist. I have known Dimitri since we were both five. He had moved directly from Greece into first grade and immediately we became incredible friends. I still remember my first school recess with him where he proved to me that people from Europe were simply by osmosis better soccer players. We shared a love of sports, music, guitars, Nintendo, Chappelle's Show, the legends of Puff and McPhee (Miss you guys, wherever you are), and various altered states of introversion.

Dimitri has always been an incredible musician who can play seemingly anything and do it quite well. I like to think I'm partially responsible since I sold him his first guitar, a cheap Grand Prix Stratocaster, for I believe $16, which played exceptionally well. I also helped destroy said guitar for no reason whatsoever in the middle of a residential road in Waterford, CT. For as good a friend Dimitri was to me, I was kind of an asshole to him.

With the aforementioned "Puff," Dimitri and I began jamming on guitar at an early age. We both improved over the years but we had never been in a formal "band" until the latter stages of Picasso Jelly when he joined during the dead man walking phase of that group to fill in for our last Webster Theatre show. It was here he met Clint and Dimitri became a natural choice as a member of *The Audience*.

Anyways, I always envied Dimitri's ear for hearing the most subtle nuance that would add so much to a song. He could hear one necessary note in a space of music and that skill always (and still) eludes me. He was also the moral conscience of the band. Not to imply that the rest of us were bad people or anything like that, but Dimitri had a certain maturity that none of us possessed.

As the bassist, he was essential at making sure I was not overplaying (I always did) and basically making sure our product was tasteful. Oftentimes, he'd tell one of us exactly what to play and he would almost always be 100% right in his recommendations. He also knew how to work and set up the PA correctly and had the largest vehicle to transport the overabundance of equipment we possessed. Lastly, his responsible nature transferred over to him not making a drunken-ass out of himself most evenings so he was almost always my ride.

With the band solid musically and possessing an evolving, yet strange collection of originals and covers, we began seeking gigs anywhere we could find them. While we did venture out to some very cool areas like playing the legendary CBGBs, the infamous "Get Your Stroh's Up" Night in Port Chester, NY that I'm still slightly hungover from, driving day and night for an incredibly weird show in the Hampton's, and playing to literally nobody at a showcase in Providence, we primarily played on the shoreline centered around the bizarre city of New London, CT.

＋——————————————————————

NEW LONDON

Ahh, ye olde Whaling City. New London is one of those classic New England/Connecticut "fake" cities that possess endless potential with little to no movement and ascent towards actualization.

All the pieces are in place. It is on the water, has solid to very good restaurants and bars, it has historical connections dating back to the Revolutionary War when Benedict Arnold went turncoat and burnt it down, and somewhat surprisingly has had a for quite some time had a very strong local music scene. There were a handful of solid places to play that had built-in crowds with people who enjoyed listening to music. Imagine that. All of these clubs had their appeal and relative strangeness about them.

Station 58 was one such club. It was an old fire station that was turned into a music venue and it was always packed. The lower level, where the fire trucks would have parked, was the "DJ" area with a bar and tables. The upper level, because that made a great deal of sense, was where the stage resided. You would have to hoof all of your gear (and in my younger musician days more gear = better) through the packed lower-level up a narrow set of stairs across the room to the stage. You got pretty good crowds, though, and it was a nice mix of males and females contrary to the typical cock-forest arrangement of most clubs.

Playing live music is a humbling experience. We had worked pretty hard to get things pretty tight and while I wouldn't say we had a following, we were getting steady work, and at a bare minimum, our name was out there. We had played Station 58 a few times already with varying success but one particular show sticks out.

We were an eclectic band of personalities and song choice was sometimes a chore. We had a solid collection of ten or so originals that were going to be played every show that was for certain. But we needed to fill more time and choosing covers became a necessity. I tended to exist in a bi-polar mindset when it came to whose songs we would play.

I loved the random songs and deep cuts from fairly obscure bands to illustrate my completely ill-perceived musical knowledge. Egotism at its finest. But, on the contrary, I also wanted to play cheesy "party-band" covers that people would dance to. My thought process was you hit them with "Living on a Prayer" right before you play a *Huffamoose* B-Side. They get their cheese; I get my nose in the air exposing the feeble peasants to good music. Suffice to say, it was never easy to come to a tacit agreement on cover songs.

Crowded House was a popular band in the mid-1980s whose biggest hit was "Don't Dream It's Over." I remembered the song from my youth but as with most music back then, didn't understand the relative complexity (deceptively simple? More on that later) of the music. Simply put, the songwriter, Neil Finn, is an incredible musician.

Clint had brought to us the idea of putting this cover into the setlist and it seemed like a great idea. The lyrics were poignant, the song drove more than you realized, and there was an inherent high-brow sophistication to bringing back a great 80s cover into a new century.

This particular show at Station 58 started quite well. The room was ¾ full, I was in my vodka-tonic gig drink phase at this point, and Mastro was relatively tuneful and subtle. After playing a handful of originals; solid ones, too, it came time for our moment of musical bougie-ness.

In those days, I was playing a Mesa Maverick amplifier and a semi-hollow body guitar and the "chime" of my tone was pretty impressive; a fairly perfect sonic palate for a big, washy 1980s tune. I remember hitting that opening D#sus and it rang out gloriously. For a moment I just knew that this track was just going to hit perfectly.

Then it happened. Just as the "deluge was being caught in the paper cup" the seas parted and the exodus began. They went in droves. It's been nearly 15 years and I remember the surrealness of that moment very clearly. I caught Clint out of the corner of my eye and saw his confusion as well. We weren't playing the song poorly; and to this day, I thought it was a good rendition. But the audience dreamt it was over and felt "liberation and release." Overdramatic as it seems, Station 58 closed shortly thereafter as the owner, whose name escapes me, abruptly skipped town, and just like that one of the cooler places in New London was gone. We helped that club "see the end of its road."

Another place we often played was Dano's Pizzeria, across the river in Groton, CT. It was a legit pizza place where we moved some tables, got some free pizza, and played long shows. Frequently, we would run out of material and replay songs from the first set in our third to run out the time and since the crowd there was nomadic, they would never know the difference.

I can still see the manager/owner, an imposing man with a 1980s mustache who did not say much. They paid very well from what I remember, so we went back even though we didn't bring much of a crowd other than drunken sailors from the nearby Sub Base. One classic gig there had the soundman get so fucked up that he passed out in his car after the first set. We had to run sound and play simultaneously. I think we played U2s "One" three times that night. Good times.

But the New London area had a myriad of venues and there were a few other interesting places on that strip that were go-to's. Bank St. Tavern (Skank St.) was a nearby dive that we played many times as part of New London band "showcases." One of the most common bands during these shows was *Degoleg*, a long-running three-piece. There was always a very strange dynamic between us and them and I'm sure we were largely to blame. They had a real solid foundation and a decent following but we were never able to get over their self-designated greatness under the moniker of being "deceptively simple." Our arrogance and egos were larger than that. And given our inconsistency, we were probably in the wrong.

Our connection with Bank St. coincided with Mastro leaving the band. Over time, while still improving as a drummer, it was clear that he was distancing himself. There were constant issues and he became progressively more detached and unreliable. Mastro's replacement was recommended to us by our friend Santucci and came with high regard. This drummer's name was Bill Pia.

Bill was a tremendous drummer with an excellent pedigree. His previous band was a hardcore punk outfit and he brought chops on top of chops to our songs. He made us "harder" and more aggressive and further opened us up to the incredible weirdness of New London.

With Mastro leaving, we also had to find a new practice spot. We used Dimitri's parents' house for a bit, then after a brief period playing in a tiny room off of a third-floor fire escape (that load-in was horrific), we were able to land the perfect spot with a rehearsal space in an in-process renovation of a commercial building on Bank Street, New London's preeminent area of prostitution. We had our own locked room that for whatever reason was being left untouched during the renovations.

It had power, but no heat, air-conditioning, or running water. Still, it provided easy access, was relatively safe and was located adjacent to Bank St. Tavern. There would be no more lugging our equipment between each rehearsal, perilous fire escapes, or hellacious icy driveways in the throes of winter. Other than my car getting plowed in the parking lot by a hit-and-run driver, it was perfect. It was here that the band began reaching its apex. And it was here we met and experienced the cast of characters that represented the deep-cuts of the New London album.

It all happened very quickly and without provocation or any semblance of warning. Mid-Spring or so in our hot rehearsal space resulted in us opening windows to avoid mass-suffocation. We must've had something worthwhile going on because lo and behold a man was crouching at our open window trying to get our attention. This man was of indeterminate age. He might have been 35 or 65. You really could not tell. He introduced himself as Ant-Man and he spoke pontificating as if he reigned supreme over the musical milieu of New London. Ant-Man spoke glowingly of his connections, his experiences as a promoter, and his purveyor-ship over the "scene." He had an answer for every question; follow-up for each answer and he quickly attempted to latch onto the band in a way that, quite frankly, did not make any sense. But we rolled with it because it just seemed fruitless to fight it and I think the circumstances were so strange and surreal that we just did not know how to adequately handle it.

His sidekick was a large man named Akita or Nikita. To this day I am not sure and we rarely spoke to him and that seemed to be to his complete satisfaction in return. They were inseparable and Ant-Man promised to be present at our next gig at a burgeoning club on Bank St. called The Oasis.

We had been to The Oasis a few times for drinks but were seemingly unaware of the large rep it was developing for live bands. As we played there more and more, we realized that it was becoming our "home" of sorts and was a definite step up from Skank St. and some of the other clubs around the city.

The stage and club were exceedingly small and narrow and as such, it would get packed out on a good night. The owner, Shawn, was an incredible guy and business owner who befriended every person he encountered and as such, his bar became one of the bright spots on the incredibly oxymoronic Bank St. strip.

Shawn was able to draw all types of bands ranging from the local heroes to national acts on the club circuit making their way to New York. There were good acts just about every night and we looked forward to our gigs there as he held a high standard for acts on his stage.

If I can say something incredibly positive about our band, it is that we are punctual as motherfuckers. Unlike bands I was in previously and have been in since, *The Audience* was going to be there early, set-up, sound checked, and three or four drinks deep by the moment the time-honored question of "when should we go on?" was first broached.

On this particular evening, we were in full-tuning mode, hours before our slated start time, when an old, rusted-out grey-black Chevy Astrovan pulled up in front of the club. If a vehicle could tell a story, this one was strung out, relapsed, and tired of the trauma it had lived through. I remember the van idling for an awkward amount of time before the passenger door flew open and the king of New London himself, Ant-Man, emerged in a bundle of energy, snow-blind from what I assume was the Peruvian adventure he had just endured.

Akita/Nikita methodically followed from the driver's side as Ant-Man made the rounds in the club and checked on the "details" that he had had absolutely no governance over. He acted as our booking agent and promoter for a gig we had booked, set up, negotiated, and orchestrated months prior. For logistical purposes, we had met Ant-Man mere days earlier. But that did not stop him from doing his thing; supervising and making sure we were taken care of regardless of our confusion and hesitant reservations.

I'm still taken aback by what he said next. After schmoozing with a very puzzled Shawn and checking out our equipment, he approached me with little regard to personal space, coke-jaw in a full circular orbit, and motioned his head toward his van. He proceeded to yell-whisper that he had some whores for when we were ready. Even as a kid, long before I truly understood the world's oldest profession, I had been taught that Bank St. had a sordid reputation. And here I was, in my early 20s, being set up, for free, by a pimp who had just become my band's de facto manager. My response is still something I think about because I don't think I have ever been caught more off-guard by a query in my life.

What follows is that one-act play.

Ant-Man: "The whores are in the van."

Me: "What?"

Ant-Man: "I've got some whores in the van for you guys. You ready?"

Me: "Pardon me?" (A phrase I don't think I had uttered before or since)

Ant-Man: "I got whores in the back. They're mostly clean."

Me: "I'm good."

Ant-Man: "Really? On me. No worries. Hand chosen. You know how I do."

Me: "Huh?"

Ant-Man: "Seriously, free. I got you. That's what you get when Ant-Man is around."

Me: "Naw. I'm good. Thanks."

Ant-Man: "Free whores. Really? Suit yourself. How about the others?"

———————————————————————————

And that was that. I immersed myself by plugging and unplugging various cables on my pedalboard pretending there was something wrong. It was a last-ditch attempt to escape from any further inquiries or suggestions about the "whores in the van" and I walk/run to the bar to do two Irish Car Bombs to cloud the memory.

Despite that initial weirdness, the show was progressing quite nicely until bizarre situation #2 reared its surreal head.

We were in the opening moments of playing an original song when a man, tall, bearded, haggard-looking, and wearing a vest of harmonicas approached us carrying a cardboard box. Now, I am not the most intelligent man nor do I have the best foresight for bad situations as indicated by my track record of poor decisions or history of passive acceptance of things that no one should passively accept. But I know this.

Never, never… Never for the people in the back, allow any person, beast, or entity to initiate a conversation with you when that being is wearing a leather harmonica vest. It's just a poor choice and to paraphrase the great Brian Fantana, 60% of the time, it goes wrong every time.

But, for the second time that day, I was floored by a situation. He introduced himself as "The Blues Dawg" and said he was here to jam with the band.

In the middle of our set. An original set at that.

Of course, he was there to jam.

He said he knew of us through Ant-Man.

Of course, he did.

He said he brought T-Shirts and a box of merch.

Of course, he did.

He said he knew BB King.

Of course, he did.

Finally, he said, "Let's do something in E."

And of course, *we* did.

I've played with some harmonica players before, including my brother, who I love very much and have enjoyed jamming with and taking the story back, one of the Romano's. But for me, the vast majority of the time playing with a harmonica player is like repeatedly biting your fork, on purpose, while getting a robust nut-tap.

Our first "jam" was an incredibly painful 1-4-5 in E minor that I think is still going. Now, I figured with a moniker (self-decreed or otherwise) like the "Blues Dawg" that you'd bring something pretty special to the table. I had visions of some "we're on a mission from God" deep soulful Chicago blues with Little Walter reincarnations aplenty.

Not quite. It was the same bends over and over and over and over... You get the picture. This jam legit took over our set, a set that we were bringing pretty strong, and we had to do an awkward, "alright! That was great!" to get him off the stage. Our conquering hero left the stage to a confused crowd and proceeded to set up his merch table for absolutely no one.

Now to rehash, in essentially a week we were befriended and inadvertently managed by a strung-out pimp named Ant-Man, were provided with subtle bodyguard/shadow service by Akita/Nikita, had turned down "mostly clean" Bank St. hookers, and now had had the pleasure to jam with the one and only, Blues Dawg. I think I do still have the t-shirt, though.

We had one more Blues Dawg encounter a few days later at an upscale club in Mystic called Latitude 41° North. This was a killer show; one in which I received a tremendous tip from a bachelorette party to "learn" "White Wedding," by Billy Idol. In actuality, that tune was already in our set and my con job was top-notch Stanislavsky method. It took me many years to tell the rest of the band about the tip I took.

Regardless, we had a nice crowd; we were having a great, great night and Mr. Dawg himself, armed with his leather assault vest, sauntered up ready to join us on a tune. This was just too much. Midsong, I told the Blues Dawg that it just was not going to happen and that our days as a sit-in blues band for his atonal harp etudes were simply over.

And oddly, that was that. Blues Dawg abruptly disappeared from our existence and gradually Ant-Man and Akita/Nikita did as well. After a few more weeks, we never saw any of the axis alliance ever again.

Sadly, the only information I ever discovered about any of the three of them was Ant-Man on Maury Povich trying to begin a relationship with his adult child and currently, him being repeatedly mugged and assaulted on the streets of New London. He is essentially a sad portrait of the continued demise of New London and emblematic of how the city still falls short of its potential. The last I heard/saw of Ant-Man was a Pagliacci-esque painting of him done to promote the city's need to take better care of its mentally disabled homeless residents.

Ironically, ridding ourselves of New London's elite coincided with the band slowly dismantling. We gave it a go as a power-trio for a bit with our slam-poet friend Mike Park trying to play bass. He was not a musician and that very quickly ended.

Later Clint took over bass duties with Dimitri moving on to drums and we played some decent shows and did some recording as a power-trio under the band name, *Your Famous Friends*. Clint, Dimitri, and I recorded much of this music, and am still quite proud of what we came up with.

But that, too, gradually faded as real-life emerged and many great plans and ideas to get the band back together notwithstanding, it just never truly clicked like that strange run in the bowels of New London.

Dimitri and I have both been on and off active doing the cover band thing in Connecticut, where sadly the money resides but even with the bigger crowds and paychecks, to me, it will just never equal that year or two running around the CT Shoreline as an original band.

The days of *The Audience* are still some of the most fun that I have had as a musician. We made some pretty cool music, drank quite a few Irish Car Bombs, got our Stroh's up, and had some incredible memories while encountering a cast of characters that were beyond surreal. So to Mastro, his girlfriend, DJ Screwface, the random New Londoners, yes, you Ant-Man, Blues Dawg,

Nikita/Akita, my friends Dimitri, Clint, Bill Pia, hell, the "mostly clean whores" and everyone else that shared the run, I thank you for the weirdness, the tunage, and the experience of feeling like a small-town hero. You really could not make it up and it remains one of my favorite experiences, music or otherwise. Rock music that rawks never stops playing through my head.

#smalltownheroes #pimpshoesmediocreshows

"Never Say Die"

I always get to the airport far too early. Usually, I use an off-site parking service, leave my car, and take a shuttle to the terminal. Without fail, when checking my car in, the attendant will look at my flight information and wonder why I have arrived so early for my flight. It's just something that I like to do.

Part of the reason is to ensure that I am never late or ill-prepared should some sort of flight shenanigans occur. And to this point, I have never missed a flight. Part of the reason is I'm a small child when it comes to airplanes. My immaturity is rooted, even at forty-one years old, in the simple fact that I love to see planes. I like the sound of the engine, the smell of the fuel, hell, I like the beeping noise from when the inter-terminal vehicles nearly kill you transporting people who are late or have mobility issues. I just love the vibe and feel of an airport. To me, there's no other place I'd rather drop $9 on a coffee and donut or scour for a quality seat to watch takeoffs and landings.

I do not travel as much as I'd like. For one, I'm a teacher and my traveling availability is generally reserved for "peak" times. And given that I find most other humans repugnant, that often throws the proverbial wrench in the plans. Another reason is that I am the proud papa to a six-year-old and while we have thus far always had fun on our infrequent plane trips, it is always a stressful experience.

This trip, though, was going to be completely different. Much to the surprise of others, I had decided to treat myself to a birthday present sans my beautiful wife and daughter and with love and respect to them both, not have to hear them speak for a few days.

And I decided I needed to go big or go home. So this was not going to be a trip to Vegas or some hyper-masculine brewery or ballpark tour. Originally, this was the idea. And of all places, Cleveland was going to be the original "getaway." I figured since I'm a musician, the Rock N'Roll Hall of Fame is a must, catch a game at Jacobs Field or whatever it's called now, and ample IPAs would do the trick. But the more I thought of it, the more that idea made me feel like I should invest in some white New Balances and ill-fitting jeans.

I thought fuck it. I have airline miles. I like warm weather and ample booze. And I'm going to make this worthwhile. Let's get weird and go solo to an all-inclusive in the Caribbean.

While plotting my options, I focused primarily on my three cheapest opportunities: the Dominican, Jamaica, and Mexico. I had been to all three previously with my wife so I was very familiar with what they all had to offer.

Jamaica was my first choice; however, I just could not get the flights to work out with my miles. The Dominican, for reasons I do not understand, was significantly more expensive, so the easy choice was to go to Mexico.

My wife and I spent our honeymoon at Maroma and it was fantastic. The sandy beaches, beautiful resorts, and pristine weather more than outweighed the inherent sketchiness of the airport in Cancun where you are immediately slaughtered by time-share reps and potential cartel members. So Mexico it was.

I arrived at the parking lot at Executive Valet a solid three and half hours early for my flight. Now maybe at a larger, busier airport, this sort of timetable would make a bit more sense. But I was flying out of Bradley International Airport in Connecticut where traffic is usually super light on even the busiest of days. Furthermore, my flight was not going to depart until about 7 am so I would be breezing through security and would more or less be sitting in a desolate terminal for at least a few hours.

As expected upon checking in, the lot attendant verified my flight information and gave me a questioning look. I nodded, goofy grin for the excitement of not only my trip but my multiple leg excursion to Cancun which included a trip on a newer American Airlines 787.

After loading my bags onto the shuttle, I took the short ride, alone with the driver to the terminal. As expected, the terminal was nearly completely deserted. In fact, given that it was before 4 am, none of the check-in counters were even "manned" yet. I had anticipated this and given my circumstances and minimalist attitude I had packed the bare minimum with just one carry-on bag to cover my four-day trip. I mean, who did I have to impress? I was there to have some drinks, get some sun, swim in the ocean, and do random solo adventures.

There were scattered people as I made my way towards security. Upon presenting my identification and boarding pass, the

TSA agent, as expected, remarked about how early I was and that my gate had not even been assigned just yet. I said I didn't mind and enjoyed the calming chaos of the terminal and made my way towards the typical American Airlines gates.

As I said before, I'm a teacher and one of my superpowers is having the ability to hold my piss for an ungodly amount of time. However, for some strange reason, when I am in an airport or train station I have an irresistible need to go to the bathroom.

Bradley is a very small airport and the Terminal is broken into two "winged" concourses of around twelve gates. As I made my way into the West concourse towards the bathroom I saw him. I try to pride myself on not being judgmental. I'm not someone who will stare and prejudge someone based upon how they look or are conducting themselves. But this guy was different.

He was angry. It was visceral and overstated yet silent anger contained solely within his body. The tension was palpable. His face was flushed and his hands were walled into fists. He wore jeans that were far too tight for his large build, thick Timberland boots, and an antiquated, Ed Hardy hoodie. He wore large, oversized Beats headphones on his head atop a beanie that had no business being worn in the middle of August. He was menacing in physical appearance alone before factoring his agitated countenance. On his back, he carried an overstuffed, red, military-style backpack

Being a little after 4 am, there were still very few people in the terminal. Still, I made sure that I avoided this gentleman at all costs. In my head, I conjured up a "nightmare" scenario of not only being on the same flight as this man but as a laugh, playing out the pantomime of him being crammed, tight jeans notwithstanding, into the middle seat next to me.

I entered and left the bathroom; wasted $9 on a coffee and blueberry glazed, and continued on my way to what I anticipated would be my gate. I found a glorious plane spotting seat at a large window watching some of the early morning corporate and business jets to New York, Boston, and DC and treated myself to a second coffee and "air donut" for sustenance.

Slowly but surely, the gate area started to fill with more and more people who arrived at sensible times for their flights. Tim Tight Jeans was nowhere to be seen and I breathed an unnecessary sigh of relief that he was angrily on another flight.

At 6:45, the incredibly obnoxious lineup in the gate area for absolutely no reason other than to block those who are trying to get on the plane process began, despite, as always, a warning not to do so by the gate agent. Since I had an awards flight, I was allowed to board in an early zone. I was inadvertently bumped into as many people as possible while passive-aggressively muttering that you are not supposed to be blocking the boarding area when your zone has not been called. But I digress.

I boarded the nearly empty plane, a newer 737 for the first leg of my flight to Philadelphia where I had a short layover and found my window seat in Row 11. I always ensure I have the window, including flights with my six-year-old, because it's my world and I want to see everything that I possibly can

I waited excitedly as people slowly but surely boarded the plane. My aisle seat was soon filled by an older woman and my eternal prayers of empty middle space may soon be realized. The plane filled up and the flight attendants began shutting the overhead compartments and the plane was being prepared for departure.

Just before the closing of the doors, another person hurriedly embarked. It was Ed Hardy Hoodie, angry and flustered as ever. He maniacally stomped his way down the aisle coming closer and closer, eyes darting row-to-row seeking his spot. It cannot be.

I concentrated on the aisle and as he got still closer I noticed that his feet and his fading Timberland's paused and pivoted at my row. Son of a bitch.

I looked up and saw a look, not of abject anger, but more of nervous frustration at this point. Perhaps he had almost missed the flight? Or was he angry due to the aisle seat? Did his jeans finally cut off circulation from his junk? Whatever it was, there was a slight change in his demeanor.

He made direct eye contact with my aisle partner and motioned with his head that he had the middle seat. I noticed, with both surprise and apprehension that he did not even consider stowing his large backpack and instead cradled it, carefully and with great tenderness, as he invaded the peace to the left. He did not, in any way, acknowledge that I existed.

I took great care not to disturb him as he was clearly in an elevated state to some degree. He fastened his seatbelt hastily and pulled it multiple times to ensure it was performing its role to his approval. He moved his backpack under his feet, careful not to draw attention from a flight attendant.

With that, we began our taxi. He was stoic and focused on the tray table on the seat in front of him as we began our takeoff roll. His right hand clutched and commandeered the shared armrest as we rotated and ascended.

It was clear he was waiting for the right moment, but it was abundantly unclear to me just what that moment was. After a tense few minutes, it happened. The seatbelt sign was extinguished and that little descending double chime was heard. You know the sound. Seconds after, a beautiful flight attendant with a southern accent grabbed the microphone to announce that we were aboard one of the brand new Wi-Fi-equipped 737s fresh to the American fleet, and that we could, with a nominal fee, connect our devices.

My first thought hearkened back to a Louis CK joke (before he was outed as a total scumbag) about airline travel, the miracle that it is to sit in a chair in the sky like a mythic Greek hero to travel to our heart's content, without fear of Oregon Trail dysentery death attacks, and that we would still complain. But this played out similar to that.

Beats boy freed our shared armrest (still slightly salty about this) from his grasp and began searching through his backpack. What followed was something truly incredible. His bag, packed with meticulous care and precision, was a techie's dream. First was the MacBook.

Being the innocuous and non-noisy person that I am, I observed with great care the dance that proceeded. He navigated to the AA Wi-Fi portal and attempted to connect. The computer lagged. His hands fidgeted and his breathing increased. Without hesitation, the MacBook was closed and replaced in his bag.

Next was a newer iPad. He logged on and again found himself attempting to connect to the plane's "new and improved" Wi-Fi. And again, 5, 6, 7, 8, lag and timed out. His breath grew deeper and more noticeable as he seemed to be vacillating between anger, frustration, and panic.

The iPad, having failed at its task, was exchanged for a Kindle Paperwhite that was equipped with a web browser. This device never stood a chance and did not even connect to the portal before it too was jettisoned.

My neighbor sat still for a few moments before going to his last hope, an older, white iPhone. The screen had seen better days and given his collection of fancy "new" technology, I was struck that he was relying on a device, arguably the most important object that was clearly past its prime.

Composing himself, he used Safari and made his way to the Wi-Fi portal yet again. This time, for reasons unknown, he connected. I'm not someone who normally believes in human energy being defined in terms of weight; heavy, light, or what have you. But this was tangible. My seatmate levitated from a weight that was slowly relieved from him. He reached into his bag, grabbed an adaptor, and plugged his oversized Beats headphones into his aging iPhone.

I looked away at this point as I felt he was quite cognizant that I was a bit out of my lane. I was careful to focus on my glorious window view as we descended into and above the clouds; the Earth diminished to insignificance below me.

It was a few moments before I noticed the music. I knew it. I knew it well. It was my childhood audibly on an aural display. Without looking over I saw Mouth not helping his father with the sink. I laughed, internally, at Chunk ruining his milkshake. I, wide-eyed and pubescent, watched Andy leading cheers in her short-shorts and leggings. This was the fucking "Fratelli Chase." Ed Hardy was watching the goddamn Goonies. And with that, the world rejoiced.

Satisfied to finally connect to his film, he obtrusively removed his hoodie to relax. He continued watching, without making a sound or peeling his eyes away from the blue light emanating from his overpriced iPhone. Cyndi Lauper sang loudly, Sloth taught us about Rocky Road, and Data unveiled his Pincers of Power. I found myself feeling great compassion for Ol' Willy and his crew trying to protect what was theirs. It was all as I remembered it, so vividly, from when I was a boy.

I found myself peering at the small screen quite frequently during the flight and I felt great solace in the sentimentality and joy it brought me. It made what was already a relatively short flight go all the more quickly and perhaps most importantly for my friends, smoothly.

In time, the double-chime returned and the flight attendant announced that all devices needed to be disconnected and stowed for our descent and eventual landing in Philadelphia. My neighbor obliged by removing his headphone cord and miraculously squeezing his phone into his painted-on jeans.

We landed without incident or celebration (God, I hate that. Don't clap, idiots) and we were even able to quickly taxi to the ramp and gate and begin the process of deplanement. I gathered my belongings, along with my neighbor and we commenced the "stand-up and wait" dance for our opportunity to disembark. He had his back to me, his Ed Hardy hoodie below him on his seat.

As he began to leave the aisle, he turned and made eye contact with me for the first time since we had sat down, casually reaching down to pick up his sweatshirt. It was then I noticed his t-shirt. It was vintage. It was glorious. It was an original "Goonies Never Say Die" tee, all black, with a skull and crossbones proudly centralized and faded.

He nodded to me and it was the only gesture that was needed. I understood. We both did. He walked with pace down the aisle, off the plane, onto the air-bridge and he was gone. And now I'm here, on a layover, HP laptop propped on a dirty counter at the Baba Bar in terminal B trying to make sense of all of this; a belligerent and unhelpful bartender gazing at the rapidity of my fingers upon the keys.

I ordered a cheesesteak, because I'm supposed to, and it is insanely mediocre. The Dogfish Head 60 minutes are doing the trick though, although I feel regret for not trying a more exotic local brew. I went for what was safe and comforting. What I knew would give me the buzz I needed to continue on my journey. What I needed to make the time tick until I was ready for something more exciting.

I saw this man, for the first time, around 4 am in Hartford and immediately disliked and feared him. I internally ridiculed his tight jeans and antiquated hoody. I questioned his quasi-hipster beanie and obvious Beats "cans." Seriously, there is so much better stuff out there. I wanted nothing to do with him and hoped that he would take any plane besides the one I was on. And now here I am.

I spent nearly two hours feeling great compassion for him. His fear, palpable and heavy, alleviated only through a movie from my youth that too brought me great solace and happiness. It's what he needed to get by and at one point in my life; it is what I needed to. I know I'll probably never see this man again and I'm sure he will never remember this experience as I will. But I think that's what makes it so meaningful to me. I saw the ether of his apprehension. I saw the rise and fall. I saw his calculable relief float from his being. I saw him keep the Goondock's alive.

#truffleshuffle #oneeyedwilliesrevenge

"Flattening the Curve"

On a mundane March 12th the board convenes

burdened with tradition and false expertise.

"Let's not follow the rest of humanity,"

the threats, clear and real, yet not present.

With zero positives, ciphered causality, and false hope,

"We must not follow through with overreaction"

declares the under reactive talking heads of state.

Time stamp: 7 pm on a heavy winter-spring night –

Two hours later we were now a part of the overreacting humanity.

Sheeping our way into mind maintenance and civil stasis.

The landscapers arrived quickly with drastic intents

That the bombastic and firm refusal is acquiesced and upended.

Earth 2020, season finale - six months premature.

An emergency meeting to prepare for a two-week shutdown

to clean, sanitize and find normality

with the full acknowledgement that routine has never been a salient

virtue.

With the bells and cattle prodding we must soldier on

in spite of the tennis and the reasons unknown.

Let's be placeholders to aid their timid minds before anxiously

anointing the clients with the plot twists of disunity.

Two weeks come and go as droplet-laden induced wildfires spread

rapidly.

And my job is to sift through the flames and save the charred

embryos for recycling.

We had no choice.

So let's find some distance and take 48 hours

to convert, assess, redesign, assess, rethink, critique

and give feedback to the feedback on the meta-rubric

so that we may sing it together, comrades:

"Let's get digital."

Enter inundations of free trials and platform diving boards

into empty concrete rebar, aggregate plastered, dry, and misused.

Lane lines established and streamlined for best practice.

Real and unreal, waterless, yet airtight.

There was no training or direction - sans expectation and without

choice.

We did what we always did.

We made it work.

And now the return engagement;

the encore presentation revealing collective emptiness and

misdirection.

If you stop asking questions, you will not be upset with our lack of

answers.

Speaking in the purest verbatim.

I could focus on what's missing the room, the people, the vibe, the

energy.

Missing my people on a level beyond cellular

only at that visceral peak can we transcend the madness.

After seventeen years, I start over.

Just like the first time.

Palms projectingly timid and sweaty,

hair askew for proper displacement

and a freshly jettisoned tie since I'm no longer a complete imposter.

Teach me again, Sir Ivan, to salivate;

To accept conditions to perceive protocol.

Instruct me on synchronicity and doubleness

as I'm voluntold to untie the constrictor bound

with simplicity, security, and harshness.

As the tech drops calls and freeze beyond recognition.

I can't bandy unprecedented without pressing the bypass button –

An addendum to my goddamn CV

under special skills and qualifications.

Flexible like a motherfucker.

Contortionism, my toxic trait.

And surrogacy, with a dash of epic emotional swings,

for the unqualified councilor.

Balancing vicissitudes and the Maytag man.

To learn to repair all that's repairable as the cork withers away

from strike to strike, hole to hole-

the dartboard is filled

#and the curve is flattened.

"Ghostwriter"

I think it's enough.

To merely contemplate

just how beautiful aging silence

permits untold appreciation

into how

#chaos begets relief.

"Denominators"

Commonality abounds in this race

with daunting left turns and altered motion.

We drift into hastened straightaways and abrupt, riotous stops.

It's the same performance –

Pitiful and expected

yet denied with the brilliance of a dirty needle.

We changed the tires with impact drivers of skepticism

and refill the tanks with heightened expectation and sudden heroic

belief.

Onto the track, we speed –

Merging amongst equals

Traversing the obscene circle and angry canyoned walls.

In time, the worn tires squeal,

exhausted fuel clings to the murky reservoir

as we fume towards the start/finish line.

In the same place where we began after banking turns and drafting

hope.

It's not different although we pretend it is.

It's the track —

the conditions the pitch, arc, and restrictors.

It's the scuffs that leave impressions

to provide numeration to what's common.

But you accelerate

for the speed still thrills the weary eyes

and catalyzes chemicals

#through your nerveless hands.

"The Power of Persuasion"

Three appeals

to the innumerable ways

we fool ourselves into thinking

that the alchemist is still stirring.

The pot filled with potential -

Vast and ancient.

As the porous wooden spoon scrapes rust filled ridges

of protective enamel-laced paint.

With three words we can find modes

to make this last forever.

Laced with claims;

Either/or illogical fallacies

of the story-truth.

#We loved with universality.

"A Snapshot of You Doing the Dishes"

I remember it.

Burned into me with harsh memory and stark regret

the dim, yellow light of the kitchen

shining down upon you as you

wash each utensil, in murky water meticulously,

with your calloused, Dawn-stained hands.

Your shoulders slumped as you knew this would be the final

dialogue,

exercised in verbal pantomime,

before you pretend to drift into sleep.

Performing mental gymnastics,

deceiving yourself into the illusion of my safety.

I knew that that lukewarm dish rack was misery to you.

#And I, selfishly aware, never offered to help.

"The Stranger in Home Depot"

You, rigid and taught, sullen, were so angry.

Tensed body, dilated hands,

fidgeting as you harassed the essential worker.

Your head on a swivel staring as I sought to seek a manager, too.

But it was different,

me, with a wide-eyed child,

perplexed at your gift for weakness.

It was the way your mask fell beneath your hardened face

as you sought a half-price sticker.

If it was a lie,

then maybe it was all worth it to put up an act to convince yourself

that only through conflict,

#you find your shallow inlet.

"Vintage"

We need new loungewear

she says with a hint of resentment and class

conveniently missing the point of peaceful reluctance.

As we put our feet up to feel at ease so

the weight may tear the shoddy threads

the new manufacturing seeks to bind.

I like my loungewear, tattered, old, comfortable –

familiarly torn to the point of touch,

yet shockingly whole to the meaning at hand.

I will always recline-

#Voraciously vulnerable and alive.

"Perhaps"

Perhaps it is within

this wondrous contradiction

that our perceptions

can finally reunite.

Perhaps it's because

of this striking hypocrisy

that the rationalization

can ultimately

#be intertwined.

"She"

I don't think she's ever truly known

just how beautiful it is to feel free.

To comprehend the comprehension

that eludes us while it resides within.

But if that's the way to her enlightenment

Then her confinement must be put in pause.

I beg of you to keep questioning

your queries and insights.

To dig beyond the know.

To taste the stalest air

and inhale the bittersweet patterns.

To know, through fog-thawing voice,

#just how loved you are.

"Moss"

If I'm here to provide stability

amongst chaotic chasms of regret

and momentous hollow realizations,

Then cling to me,

my textured moss,

to muse and meander like weathered stone

#Into the runoff of spirit.

"The Most Terrifying Feeling in the World"

The most terrifying feeling in the world –

Coercive, insentient, and strangely coquettish

is the thought that misery becomes a conscious choice.

A spiritual paralysis

bent on preventing the tenderness

Of complete

#vulnerability rocking them to the core.

"Patience Stands Still"

Here's the restless renowned meaning

Of patience standing still

While the coalesced commanding satire

Still bends beyond its will

You tell me complacency reside within

All along hew stained walls that speak

In a false minute's sultry sin

Targeted heart and soul that resides incomplete

Love lies starving

when hysterical loneliness lies in hysterics.

Missing the lines of the measure,

we cannot compute the meaning,

single, double, repeat of being truly alone

#until we sever the threads that weaves us into knots.

"A Second"

Let's take a second to admonish –

just how beautiful it is

that the red lights of foreign steel

reveal our intense fragility.

Let's just take a second to decipher-

just how powerful it is

to reflect on every minute, second and moment,

with recommendation that the multitudes

#bow to your false recollection.

"Crane"

Say these are merely lines,

an assemblage of terse words

that we used to justify

why do we feel so hurt?

So let us all be realists,

held back by some criticality.

Yes, it's a concept

#Critiqued by our desire to feel consequential.

.

"Complicate"

Let's complicate what it is to make meaning

in such subtle movements.

A leveled attack

amongst acute angles of connection.

Let's allow this shit to soar,

obscenity or not,

calculating the percentage of our favor.

Anxious understandings amidst relevancy.

the true damage

resides

#not without but within the delivery of the promise.

"The First Time"

There was a first time

where I witnessed the acidic nature

of a vinegar, healthful, reformative, disgusting

Prove to you, the beauty that emanates beyond you

But yet, as revolting as it seems

I will make you sick to ascertain

just how beautiful you are.

Yet still within that ruination

#do you seek more validation from me?

"...all good apologies end in a #ashtag"

Maybe we are just wired differently.

Voices beaming forth with obtuse tones to reveal.

What?

A story of two people.

Names invisible and perceptible

when we are all the same.

They meet covertly.

They fall in love with clandestine atmospheres

and develop something beyond meaningful.

They tremble, they shiver.

They wipe the minuscule granules of sand that calloused their skin.

And they live.

In happiness, perhaps.

Perhaps perseverance or endurance is the correct term

Trapped inside some sort of digital frontier that both creates and

debilitates

All that they have once cherished

conjoined by the rapture of the blue light.

An escape that proves too well

that to define oneself we must have a self that is worth defining.

That we coalesce hidden

within androgynous algorithms and

#the burdens of hope.

"Four A.M. on the Sand"

Secretly I found you,

Four A.M. on the sand.

As the fog danced around you

as uncertainty evolved unplanned.

Who knew that trembling could be so meaningful?

This is all I cherish

when I'm caught within your glance.

With such beauty and resplendentness

magnetism reacts, and advance.

In such perfect symmetry,

the skin shivers deep,

and the secret is uncovered.

With a song for your body to exhale, relapse, and face release.

A song for your body as the cold traverses in through the REM sleep.

A song for your body to let the past transfix its way right through

you.

A song for your body it's the least, the least, the least that I could do.

You are electricity shocking the death from within me;

as life slowly beckons.

Yet in such simplicity,

#I find everything right in front of me.

"When I am Old"

When I am old,

lost in reminiscence and regret

foolishly holding on to the things I'd like to forget.

When I am old,

caustic and bitter, stammering

still half looking for a sheepish angle inside my fading will.

When I am old,

slow handed arthritic hands of the past

fingers clawing the discordant memory of the moments that did not

last.

There you will be –

Still young and vibrant,

atomic and pure.

Innocence abounds in an observant stature.

Blonde, catalytic energy coursing through your veins

where a green smile of youthful intensity

surmounts, succumbs, satisfies and delivers life

To me.

When I am old.

Still pure

Innocence abound in an observant stature

Blonde catalytic energy coursing through your veins

Where a green smile of youthful intensity

Surmounts, succumbs, satisfies

And delivers life

To me...

#When I am old.

"Pedagogy"

A teacher.

In the beginning, is to be a learner

wide-eyed innocence

soaking up the knowledge provided to you.

For you.

With best practice and genius scaffolded and constructivist.

And Wong and Marzano and Burke and Beers and a case of

bourbon, too.

To schedule your Pre, Post, During

coupled with an anticipatory set

to mobilize the milieu and edubabble.

We assemble according to protocol and understand by design.

That is until your first student pretends

To snap his neck with an empty tic-tac container

Cracking and falling in full view

to prove he's in charge.

Student-centered, for sure.

And that's how it goes.

#At least I have an organized filing cabinet.

"Adventures of a Selfie"

Take 27.

I believe because I'm conditioned

to add more tilt, adjust the aperture,

stall the shutter, interrogate the ISO.

To make this artificially organic,

without the darkness permeating the light.

My vision, solely based,

on an allusion to painted images I've never seen or mirrored.

Take 28.

Just post it, liberate it, unfiltered, and charming.

Act naturally within my skeletal form and justify the joyful noise.

Submit, post, and dirty delete.

In the most unnatural state of delusion.

#we create our most authentic conclusion.

"Sordid View"

I can't interpret the interpretations.

I can't feel the warmth of today,

if I can't let the feeling go.

I just read the lines from above.

The voice proves so meaningful

as solace echoes flow.

Suddenly the night grew oh so still

pacified by the whistling wings

singing of a lost melody

Where the colors sound no warning

with a stringent resound weights as light as day.

Soothing dissonance sounds out of control.

I'm begging to heal

as the opaque images fall from idle imagination.

I'm looking forward to the day where I can finally say

that I'm finally moving on.

To look back upon all this

with some simple subtle willingness

to remember to forget.

I'm beginning the restoration

from this sordid view of starving, creativity overcomes.

But still I know

that seamless urges come and go.

I bear the scars from them all

with hollow words that cleanse my soul.

Organized so I'll part

with the countless beginnings that I've lost.

Just to venture to start again with

#the dream I have sought.

"Still Awakening"

A still awakening,

with subtlety so effortless beside me.

My fingers dance upon your skin.

If I could map out every contour,

to define your geography.

It's in this moment I am truly happy

In soft minutes lies this guarantee

to understand what was meant to be

relies on you seeing it, too.

Torn, lost, in your ghost,

the skeletal blueprint just does me in.

We blindly stare into vulnerability

#to happily drown in this excess.

"Salute"

I'll raise a glass as the walls come crashing down.

It's not so easy to be sincere.

It takes mere seconds for me to surmise

that the shadow-less glance trapped in your eyes

was worth something so true.

Let's torch the bridges past

as smoke-filled rings form from your velvet lips

#to sing the colors of elusiveness.

"Chance"

A chance in many crimson sunsets

walked three miles toward the cracks

that separates my happiness

further still it's what I lack

It's a robotic sensibility

To hone these defaults

Of patent images that I conjure up

not knowing where to start

But infinite one I see you

lying naked in my arms

if only this were true

It's a step toward familiarity

past the ghost of this dream

cut my skin just a bit more

maybe it's just passion that I bleed

So I'd like to tell you a story

a story of how I got like this

curse the shadows of my madness

#how you could erase it with a kiss.

"Hiding Away on the Inside of the Jacket"

It's there for the world to see.

To judge and conjure

if the words written by this vacant face

equate to the thoughts that are truly in this head.

What do you see?

The photo is authentic but the look in the eyes.

Hollow and degrading?

Self-aware to the critical gaze

#upon the lines of a stranger.

"Everyone Else was Grieving"

I wasn't happy.

But I never truly understood why we raced there so fast.

The breakdown lane,

a violent conduit just to say goodbye

to a jaundiced, yellow, at-last at peace, body.

Truthfully, you had been gone for ages.

Fighting a battle heroic and true,

but fruitless in its attrition.

Around me the anguished cries,

tears rolling down pale, ashen faces

devoid of recollection, realism, and relief.

Everyone else was grieving.

But I was not.

I was relieved without selfish, theatrical acts

or outward emotive release.

Finally, I knew the ringing of the phone

would no longer hold your purpose,

that your energy would be encased,

#without confinement, soaring above that hill.

"Milestone #3"

It was that moment that most yearn for

except for when the vision is presented.

Since you cannot surmise the nature of fear

until you've seen her eyes stare through your invisible presence.

Yet, this experience of awkward accomplishment

and success reigns true.

I parented to this instance.

#And this too, I sort of survived.

"Addiction"

I need.

With frightened eyes and attuned ears,

acute and omnipotent, withering feet

cautiously de-stepping down creaking stairs towards the darkness

below.

Grasping my alarmed-prepared phone,

I wait to hear the rustling

from your deaf all-knowing ears

to provide for me just one more day.

Voice and body, paralyzed and atrophied,

#your tail still wags.

"Ligature"

When the patterns wear thin from vague overuse

and constructed narratives,

that's where we find ourselves.

Stuck and languishing.

We're not imposters if we control the plot.

Hastily tethering ligature to the leitmotif

and manipulating synthetic metaphors.

That's not overt, ornamented or spurious.

#That's a true connection.

"Four Pages in March"

I started writing a book.

On March 1st it was so true and meaningful,

A day later it proved an opening of my soul.

I needed it more than I could ever calculate.

By the fourth day, it held empty weight like a to-do list

That we willfully ignore.

But the list lies heavy and is all but a necessity.

March is not the longest month, but it's the month I choose to forget

Like those meaningful words that I surrendered to the air.

#Breathless and free; the book spans four pages.

"Blackout"

I used to fiend the escape

From people I never cared about and still don't

Who would elucidate about how much I was content

When I was trying to diminish from who I was

And become something unconscious.

The bitter irony

So unwilling to accept

That when I lose sense of myself

#I am what others wish I could be.

"Frame"

I keep four pictures on my stained

desk containing your face

in varying phases of development, smile, and awe.

You are everything to me.

Each enduring day, I stare and elicit purpose.

But I prepare to greet you

with impatient correction and hypercritical glance.

You are six.

Truth is conditional and maniacal.

Under your anxiety is a person,

a child, a human, who has stopped feeling whole.

In part, because of me.

And still,

I return to the novelty frames, smiles of the past,

and think that those forced paint-by-number

moments are still within my artist's palate.

Maybe.

I can still ascertain,

someday,

that your smile today is based upon relief.

That you have learned not that the acrylics

may stain your hesitant fingers,

#but that the hues can formulate legitimacy.

"Bridges"

I wrote a letter that I instantly regret

and all those words I bled out of fear, out of pretense.

I wouldn't take any of them back.

I thought it would all fall apart

with quickness, and resolve so I could revel in your demise.

I plotted to burn the bridges

with combustible sparks of egotism and parallel structure.

I enjoy the flames of watching others

turn me into fragile kindling and sadistic, waning ash.

The abstract, the mundane,

#the concrete and ethereal is truly gone.

"Independence Day"

It was during a mediocre movie that I was forced to say goodbye.

Not by choice but by a bypassed spiritual adorned necessity.

You stood ready and perhaps we shared

the subtle reality that time had just passed.

In retrospect, the movie made sense

in its Pourquoi-laden plot of obvious tendencies

and melodramatic mirroring of self.

We knew the aliens would come.

We knew they would rally together

and we knew, in the end, we would move forward "stronger."

With purpose and didactic equivocation for substitute emotions.

The script has been on my stage for ages

with platitudes and idiomatic sensibility.

But I swear, you died when Judd met Jeff.

And his words, richly constructed with sardonic sentimentality, detailed your pride.

I beamed and felt those notions at that moment, knowing

but not knowing as sweat cloyingly dripped from my escape

that it was you speaking to me then,

through the mouthpiece of a man, we watched together.

When, as a child, I feigned sleep to hear your laughter.

Up far past my bedtime under the glow of aged reruns

to connect to a man I so envied and loved.

You said it to me then as your last breaths

emanated from your tired being as you had

when you thought you had needed to years prior.

That night, I saw you lifeless, robed, and incubated on a gurney

mouth agape, skin ague, and life alienated.

I knew you had loved and lived and your exhaustion erupted

volcanically

like the Kilauea you so adored.

The snow fell with aggressive abandon upon my car that night as I traversed an interstate filled with temerous eyes.

White-knuckled upon a pleather cover,

I traveled freely through without fear or consternation.

My car, gliding from lane-to-lane,

salt deposits on road, steel, and skin guiding me "home"

to face a newly closed door, hypercritical rationalization, and your

granddaughter.

Her face memorializing your Groucho impression, googly-eyes, and

generosity.

Our independence was now complete.

We were unfettered and united in the multitudes

free to be gathered in wind-swept greenery and chance.

I held her fretful hand to speak softly to her,

to shush her fragile psyche into sleep.

She understood that she was honored to remember you forever.

To be independent of her Papa but dependent

#upon the pride you had bestowed.

"In a Hoarder's Living Room in Connecticut"

I once laughed so hard I lost consciousness in a hoarder's living room

in Connecticut. My glasses fell to the dirty carpet

weighed down by emotion and happiness.

From the corner of my eye, I saw your face reveling in a moment.

You were yourself.

You're still here, in title and description,

but emotionally the ether ensconced your spirit

and eviscerated the laughter that permeated between us.

It was never your fault.

Yet you bear the carriage and the sickness.

I miss it.

Days of mashing buttons as the Winamp symphony

out-sensed the grease of our fried-food.

I've rarely seen you in many years.

At least as it was in those cherished moments

as your physical being is reduced to a shadowy depression.

Your insight clouded by anxious agitation

and restless regurgitation of burdened maladies.

You're still my protector,

my vicariously living being

who taught me about Superfly Snuka,

Queen albums sped-up and spun backward,

and Rockette Morton running on laser beans.

I feel your pain,

but like an oven self-cleans the remnants of sustenance memory,

I am left with a sanitized stench of what once was.

I regained consciousness that day,

tears of laughter streaming down my flushed, crimson face.

In a hoarder's living room in Connecticut,

I picked up my glasses from the filthy, debased carpet

and I realize now, that perhaps, I saw you with 20/20 vision.

Perfection in its way.

But maybe, what I see now,

torturously and with reluctance is much more important.

Pained authenticity coupled with burdened strength.

#It is you now.

"Parallel Lines and Structures"

I've learned the weight of the silence of your words

Rippling the melancholic ether with tings of resentment.

It didn't have to be this way - the distance between infinity

Begetting parallel lines and structures.

But it did,

And I'm still not sure why.

If this is not what you wanted, what we created,

or imagined, it still is what has occurred and in that we cannot deny.

This is true.

This is also untrue.

The story within the story will always reveal

Omission within that sordid script and the revisions cast,

outline

A hollow shadow amongst

Magical movements and enharmonic songs.

I still believe

Maybe I shouldn't.
But I know no other way since the silence,
ripe with humidity And tension filled kinesthetics,
still feels magnetic and painfully ethereal.

It's funny that the semantics of love,
torn, fluid
and nutritious to the point
Of starving sustenance,
can also sadly be the basis for
#the narrative that disavows the truth.

"Facing the Humble Horizon with Then and Now"

I held my six-year-old self tightly as a ring of fire emerged from the
humble horizon.
It was surprisingly simple.
The little-one needed to feel secure, without fears of abandonment.
Disentangled from the pre-emptive panic of loss.
I embraced him, lovingly, with reassurance and strength;
With words of meaning and truth-told rampant hypocrisy.

To be secure from abandonment, I told him,
Is to know that you are truly safe.
Now.
And, in retrospect,
Then.

I spoke with tears streaming down my aging face,
Caught briefly in my periorbital puffiness
aligned with years of caustic repudiation.
Mostly of my own doing.
Mostly constituting, my undoing.

I kindly advised to open his core, unlock the cage, and allow the

hateful doves

Of years past escape their constrained box

To haplessly journey freely towards that eclipsing sun.

Past the line of sea-tossed shells that boundaried the shore,

Past the dilapidated jetty where I sat and gazed longingly,

Past the memories of the pain of that hateful self

That had, for so many years, attempted to protect me.

I'm not angry anymore.

I'm empathetic.

And tired.

Exhausted from holding back a piece of me

To protect the piece of me from that feeling of unity.

I told my six-year old self to close and lock his rib cage

And hold what matters most within him.

To emerge

#Safe from Then, to be prepared for Now.

"Parados"

What I remember most
Is the way the yellow ring of your eyes
Formed the parados of your being.

They shined, they trembled, and
colored the silent simplicity
#With the stark fragility of hope.

"Umbrella"

Under a flimsy umbrella on an asshole's patio, I first knew you.
You were timidly extroverted extolling your violent introspect.
We conversed of starving love, life, hate, pain,
Amidst the obscure psychological riddles of double entendre and

pun.

I loved you in that momentary haze.
An eminence of glow, resplendent and pure,
danced upon the medallion flame
Of your persistent aura.

You were hurting within, without, and the burn
Of your visceral scars, sang through
the voice erupting from your freckled skin.

There was something infinite about the way you twanged
The consonants of your past.
Something forever about the way you embraced the suffering air
#Amidst the heat and tension of that June afternoon.

ABOUT THE AUTHOR

Brian Wilcox was born and raised in the amazingly strange Nutmeg State, Connecticut. He is a public school educator and weekend warrior musician who still thinks he could be a rock star. Brian values family more than all else and when not playing renditions of disco and funk in a random bar on a Friday or Saturday, can be found spending copious amounts of time with his amazing wife, daughter, and senile dog and cat. ...*all good apologies end in a #ashtag* is his first collection of writing.